TOO Small Tola

Gets Tough

Other books by Atinuke

Too Small Tola
illustrated by Onyinye Iwu

Too Small Tola and the Three Fine Girls
illustrated by Onyinye Iwu

Anna Hibiscus
illustrated by Lauren Tobia

Good Luck, Anna Hibiscus!
illustrated by Lauren Tobia

Hooray for Anna Hibiscus!
illustrated by Lauren Tobia

For younger readers

Baby Goes to Market
illustrated by Angela Brooksbank

B Is for Baby
illustrated by Angela Brooksbank

Catch That Chicken!
illustrated by Angela Brooksbank

Baby, Sleepy Baby
illustrated by Angela Brooksbank

Hugo
illustrated by Birgitta Sif

Nonfiction

Africa, Amazing Africa: Country by Country
illustrated by Mouni Feddag

TOO Small Tola

Gets Tough

ATINUKE

illustrated by

ONYINYE IWU

CANDLEWICK PRESS

For every child who went through lockdown
A

To anyone who has sacrificed their education
and childhood to help their family financially.
We salute you.
OI

Text copyright © 2022 by Atinuke
Illustrations copyright © 2022 by Onyinye Iwu

First US edition 2023
First published by Walker Books Ltd. (UK) 2022

Library of Congress Catalog Card Number 2022936947
ISBN 978-1-5362-2946-2

22 23 24 25 26 27 LBM 10 9 8 7 6 5 4 3 2 1

Printed in Melrose Park, IL, USA

This book was typeset in Stempel Schneidler.
The illustrations were created digitally.

Candlewick Press
99 Dover Street
Somerville, Massachusetts 02144

www.candlewick.com

CONTENTS

\\l//

\\l//

\\l//

Dapo Grandmommy Tola Moji

Trouble for Too Small Tola

Tola lives in a run-down block of apartments in the megacity of Lagos, in the country of Nigeria. She lives with her grandmother, who is very bossy; her sister, Moji, who is very clever; and her brother, Dapo, who works very, very hard.

Some say that more than twenty million people also live in Lagos.

There are billionaires with private helicopters to take them to Mecca every Friday.

And there are people with no bank accounts. If they miss one day of work, they cannot buy food that day.

Tola and her family are lucky. Tola's brother, Dapo, has a job as a mechanic. And they can buy as much food as they need!

Dapo earns so much that Grandmommy does not need to work selling groundnuts by the side of the road like she used to do. Now Grandmommy can stay at home and chat with the neighbors who live in the other rooms in the block of apartments. And now Tola can go to school every day instead of having to help sell groundnuts sometimes.

Tola loves school! And when she comes home, there is always food ready. And food is even packed for Mrs. Shaky-Shaky too.

Mrs. Shaky-Shaky is a neighbor who is too shaky to cook for herself. So Grandmommy often packs food for her. All the neighbors do.

"Come and eat," Grandmommy says to Tola every day when she gets home. "Eat and then you can concentrate on your schoolwork."

And every day Tola hugs Grandmommy. It is so good to eat. So good to have time for homework.

One evening, Tola opens her math notebook. She loves how numbers fit together like a puzzle—a puzzle that you can put together and then take apart again.

She stares at the pages where she has written her times tables. And suddenly, Tola sees the answers to division problems!

"Moji!" Tola shouts.

Tola's sister, Moji, does not look up from her borrowed school computer. Moji has a scholarship to a fine-fine school. She is determined to become a doctor.

Grandmommy says, "Tola, do not bother your sister!"

4

Grandmommy is determined that Moji become a doctor too. Then they will be able to live in a proper house with several rooms and have a cook and a washerwoman.

But Tola is too excited to be quiet!

Inside the equation 3 x 12 = 36 she can see the answer to the problem 36 ÷ 12! And also the answer to 36 ÷ 3!

Tola is sure of it. She shrieks and claps her hands.

Moji frowns.

"What is it?" she asks at last.

"Multiplication and division are the same!" Tola crows. "But backward!"

Moji smiles.

"Show me!" she says.

So Tola writes:

3 x 12 = 36

36 ÷ 12 = 3

36 ÷ 3 = 12

3 x 12 = 36
36 ÷ 12 = 3
36 ÷ 3 = 12

"You are right, little sister!" Moji smiles again. She looks up at Grandmommy and says, "Maybe this one could get a scholarship too!"

Tola's eyes become as wide as the pans Grandmommy used to fry groundnuts. Could this be true?

But just then somebody starts shouting in the corridor outside their room, and Grandmommy hurries out.

"A scholarship, Moji?" Tola asks with her eyes still wide.

Dapo laughs. He is resting on the bed after his long day bent over the open hoods of broken cars.

"What is it with you and school?" he asks. "Other girls like to think about fashion and hair and boys and babies—"

Moji snorts. "It is you who likes to believe girls think about fashion and hair and boys and such because you want girls to be pretty and think about nothing but you!" she says.

Dapo's mouth opens and closes like a fish. Tola giggles.

"But you know nothing about girls!" Moji concludes.

Dapo narrows his eyes, but before he gets the chance to speak, shouts come through the open window.

"Da-po! Da-po! Da-po!"

Dapo smiles and swings his legs down from the bed. He leans out of the window.

"How far?" he asks. "Wha's up?"

"We are losing!" a boy shouts back.

"I beg, come play for us!" shouts another.

Dapo laughs. "I work now," he says. "I tire too much to play football."

There is a chorus of disagreement. But Dapo shakes his head again.

"I cannot play now," he says. "I am the man of my house."

Dapo turns away from the window—just in time to see Moji roll her eyes.

"Wha's your problem?" he asks.

"Man of the house?" Moji says. "You are only fifteen!"

"So?" Dapo sucks his teeth. "Who paid for that phone sitting next to you?"

Moji used to be the only one in her class without a phone. And the other girls mocked her for it. When Dapo found out, he had worked overtime for weeks until he could buy a phone for Moji.

Moji stares down at her phone now. She bites her lip and says, "Sorry, Dapo."

Tola's mouth falls open. She has never heard Moji apologize to Dapo before!

"No problem." Dapo beams.

He is grinning as if he has just won *Nigeria's Got Talent*!

Tola stares at them. There are hidden equations in life as well as in math, Tola realizes.

Grandmommy stomps back into the room.

"People say there is a new sickness. Mama Business is sure it will kill all of us. Foolish woman!"

Moji, Dapo, and Tola look at one another.

"The virus?" Moji asks.

"Boss says this illness is only abroad," Dapo says.

"No," Moji argues. "Plenty of people are sick here too—plenty-plenty."

"But Teacher said the virus cannot come here," Tola protests. "He says our strong sun will finish it completely!"

Grandmommy stands with her hands on her hips. She says crossly, "So my own grandchildren know about this killer illness— but you left it to Mama Business to tell me?"

Moji, Dapo, and Tola look down, shamefaced.

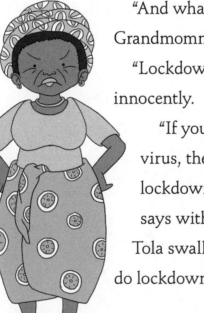

"And what about lockdown?" Grandmommy demands.

"Lockdown?" Tola asks innocently.

"If you know about the virus, then you know about lockdown," Grandmommy says with narrowed eyes.

Tola swallows. "Abroad they do lockdown," she says slowly.

"Governments shut people in their houses so they cannot run around spreading the illness," Dapo joins in.

"How?" Grandmommy snorts. "How can the governments lock people for house? What about their work? If they do not work, then how will they eat?"

"In London, people do not need to work in order to eat," Moji says eagerly. "They have banks full of money!"

"London ko, London ni." Grandmommy waves her arms. "What about here in Lagos? If lockdown come, how will people eat?"

"I don't know, Grandmommy," Dapo says, opening his palms wide.

Grandmommy sucks her teeth and everybody keeps quiet. Now that Grandmommy is cross, anything anybody says could just make her crosser.

Moji's phone pings. Tola reads the message as it flashes across the screen.

"A party!" she cries.

"What party?" Grandmommy frowns deeply.

"I don't know," Moji says, staring at her homework.

Grandmommy snatches up Moji's phone to look. Moji is not allowed a password.

Tola sees over Grandmommy's shoulder a photo of two girls wearing very thick makeup and very short skirts.

"What?" Grandmommy shrieks. "Are these girls from your school? How can their parents allow them to leave the house looking like this?"

"I don't know," Moji says again, still staring at her computer screen.

"No granddaughter of mine," Grandmommy bellows, "is going to a party with girls who look like this! You hear me, Moji? I forbid you to go!"

"Good," Moji says. "I was not going anyway. I have work to do."

Grandmommy blinks several times. Then she bangs Moji's phone back down on the table and marches out of the room, muttering.

"Thanks, Tola," Moji grumbles. "Who asked you to read my messages?"

"Sorry, Moji," Tola says.

More messages ping into Moji's phone. She does not look up. But Dapo does. He whistles at the photos of the girls.

"Moji," Dapo says slowly, "this party looks fun."

"Fun for who?" Moji asks.

"For you!" Dapo says. "How about you have some fun for once?"

"I have work to do," Moji says.

"Come on! I want to go!" Dapo comes clean. "Take me to this party, Moji! I beg you!"

Moji looks up from her homework in surprise.

"You are joking?" she asks.

"Why?" Dapo frowns. "Is your own brother not good enough to go to your fancy school parties?"

"Don't say that, Dapo!" Moji exclaims. "I just don't want to go."

"What about lockdown?" Dapo asks. "This could be the last party for . . . forever!"

"Lockdown!" Moji snorts. "You heard Grandmommy—nobody can lock down Lagos."

"So go for me!" Dapo says. "Come on, for your brother who works from morning to night so you can go to school. For your brother who worked overtime so he could buy you a phone . . ."

Moji groans and puts her head in her hands. But she says, "OK, OK, OK!"

Dapo leaps off the bed as if he has scored a goal.

Tola's eyebrows shoot up her forehead. Here are more equations she had not foreseen!

Tola watches in astonishment as Moji and Dapo pull boxes out from under the bed where Grandmommy keeps all their best clothes.

"Grandmommy will kill you," Tola says slowly.

"We will be back before she knows anything!" Dapo says.

"But what if we have lockdown?" asks Tola. "What if you can't get home?"

Dapo pretends not to hear her.

Just as they are leaving, Moji grabs the food for Mrs. Shaky-Shaky.

"Tell Grandmommy we have gone to take food to Mrs. Shaky-Shaky," she says. "Tell her we will visit Mrs. Shaky-Shaky for some time."

Tola nods slowly.

When Grandmommy comes back, Tola has tidied the whole room. Now she is on the bed writing out all the division problems she can see in the multiplication tables.

Grandmommy does not seem to notice that Moji and Dapo are not there.

"A virus, a killer virus . . ." she mutters.

Tola looks at Grandmommy. She is not cross, Tola realizes. She is worried.

"Don't worry, Grandmommy," Tola says. "The heat will kill the virus."

Grandmommy sits down with a grunt.

"Where are Moji and Dapo?" she asks suddenly.

"They took Mrs. Shaky-Shaky's food," Tola says, staring down at her notebook.

Grandmommy nods. She picks up a piece of paper from the table and fans herself with her eyes closed.

Tola lets out a deep breath. She lies down on the bed and lets her eyes droop. Tola can rearrange equations even with her eyes closed . . .

"Tola!" Grandmommy shouts suddenly.

Tola's eyes fly open. The sky is dark outside the window. It is night. She must have fallen asleep while counting.

"Where are Moji and Dapo?" Grandmommy asks.

Tola looks around, blinking.

Moji should be asleep next to her in the bed. But she is not. Dapo should be asleep on his mat on the floor. But he is not either. Suddenly, Tola remembers where they went.

"Moji's bag is not here," Grandmommy says. "Why did Moji take her bag to Mrs. Shaky-Shaky?"

"I don't know, Grandmommy," Tola says, twisting her mouth down.

Grandmommy eyes Tola.

"Did they ask you to lie for them?" she asks.

"No, Grandmommy," Tola whispers.

"So why are you lying for them?" Grandmommy shouts.

Tola's mouth starts to tremble. Then she starts to cry.

Grandmommy sighs loudly, shaking her head. "Stop crying," she says to Tola. "This is not your trouble."

Tola tries to stop crying. She tries to go back to sleep. But she is too worried about what is going to happen now.

Grandmommy stands looking out of the window toward the road. Her foot is tapping. After a long time, she moves to wait by the door.

Then Tola hears footsteps in the corridor. She hears Dapo laugh. She hears Moji shush him.

"We have to creep in," she hears Moji whisper. "So when Grandmommy wakes up, she will find us in our beds."

Tola rolls her eyes. Moji is clever at computer work. But not so clever at life.

Then the door opens. There are Dapo and Moji looking so fine in their best clothes.

Grandmommy pounces and grabs their ears.

"Please, Grandmommy!" Dapo begs. "We took food to Mrs.–"

"You think I was born yesterday?" Grandmommy shouts. "Don't even try to lie to me. I know where you were!"

"Sorry, Grandmommy!" Moji wails.

"Sorry ko, sorry ni!" Grandmommy shouts. "Wait until tomorrow—then you will be sorry! Tomorrow I will punish you!"

Moji weeps and Dapo wails.

But when morning comes, it brings bigger things to worry about than one night of disobedience.

They wake to hear all the neighbors out in the corridor shouting at once.

"What is it?" Grandmommy runs to open their door.

"Lockdown," Mrs. Abdul sobs.

"Lockdown is here!" Mrs. Raheen wails.

Tola and Moji and Dapo sit up and look at one another.

"Lockdown," Tola whispers.

"Lockdown!" Moji gasps.

"Lockdown," Dapo moans.

"Weytin be lockdown?" Mrs. Shaky-Shaky is perplexed.

"Everybody has to stay for house," Mama Business explains. "No person allowed to go to school or work or market."

Grandmommy throws her hands up in the air.

"How will people get money for food if they no go work?" she shouts.

"Government wants us to choose between virus and hunger!" Mr. Abdul bursts out.

"If one does not kill us, then the other will!" Mrs. Raheen shakes her head.

At this thought, Grandmommy starts to pray. And Mr. Abdul and everyone else joins in. It does not matter that some people are praying to Jesus and other people are praying to Allah. They all pray together.

They pray not to be forgotten when the world's problems come. They pray that those who have money in the bank will remember those who do not. They pray that the virus will pass quickly and take not one person with it.

At last, Grandmommy comes back into the room.

"What about school?" Moji whispers.

"School?" Dapo shouts. "What about my work? How will we eat?"

"I will sell groundnuts!" Grandmommy says firmly.

It is how she has always looked after them when there is no other way.

"But you are not allowed!" Tola wails.

Grandmommy tightens her lips.

"Who is going to stop me feeding my children?" she asks.

"The police," Moji whispers.

"Let them try!" says Grandmommy, rolling up her sleeves.

Now Tola is frightened.

"No, Grandmommy!" she cries.

Suddenly, a loud car horn sounds from outside. Dapo looks out. He can never ignore a car, no matter what else is going on.

Dapo whistles. "BMW!" he says. "Is that not your principal, Moji?"

Moji runs to the window. Tola peeps out too. There is a big black BMW parked on the rough ground. A fine woman is standing next to it looking toward their building.

"Yes!" Moji exclaims. "It is Teacher!"

"Moji—what did you do?" Grandmommy frowns.

"Nothing!" Moji protests.

"Are you in trouble?" Grandmommy persists.

"No, Grandmommy!" Moji insists.

"So why is your teacher here then?" Grandmommy asks.

"I don't know!"

Moji runs out of the room. Grandmommy hurries after her.

Tola watches out of the window as the teacher talks to them. Then Moji runs back into the building.

"Teacher has come to collect me," she says when she bursts into the room.

"Why?" Tola and Dapo ask together.

"So I can live in her house. Then I can use her internet and continue my schooling during lockdown."

Tola stares at Moji.

"Live with your teacher?" Tola asks.

"Yes," says Moji, snatching up her books and her clothes.

"When will you come back?" Tola asks slowly.

"When school reopens," Moji says.

"When is that?" Tola asks.

But Moji only shrugs and rushes out, clutching a bag of her possessions.

"Moji!" Tola shouts.

"Teacher says I have to hurry before the police close the roads."

Moji rushes away without saying goodbye. Tears well up in Tola's eyes.

She watches Moji get into the back of the BMW.

When Grandmommy comes back in, she sits down heavily. She passes a hand over her face.

Nobody says anything.

Then Dapo shouts, "Boss!" and dashes out of the room.

"Who now?" Grandmommy frowns.

Tola looks out of the window. She sees Dapo run out of the apartments toward a short, fat man. The man puts his hand on Dapo's shoulder while he talks to him.

Uh-oh, thinks Tola.

Soon Dapo bursts back into their room.

"Boss say I should go and sleep at work. Then we can continue fixing cars for doctors and people who are still allowed to drive around," he announces.

"No, Dapo!" Tola cries—everybody is going, everybody is leaving her.

"Dapo—" Grandmommy says.

"I will send you money!" Dapo shouts, and runs out of the door.

Tola starts to cry.

Grandmommy smiles a wavering smile.

"Don't cry for Dapo!" she says. "Did you not see how fast he ran? He loves cars so much he wants to sleep with them!"

Tola chokes on her sobs. She is giggling at the thought of Dapo sleeping with one arm around a car.

Then she sees Grandmommy pass a hand over her face again. Tola comes to stand beside her.

She wishes Moji and Dapo had not gone. They did not even have one last night together! She puts her hand on Grandmommy's arm. Grandmommy looks down at Tola's hand.

"Dapo needs to work and Moji needs to continue her schooling," Grandmommy whispers. "Their prayers have been answered."

Then she looks at Tola. "What about you?" she asks. "What do you pray for?"

Tola rests her cheek against Grandmommy's arm.

"To stay with you . . ." she says. "And also to find all the equations in life."

Then Grandmommy chuckles. She puts her arms around Tola. And Tola hugs her back!

Too Much for Tola

Too Small Tola is on lockdown in a run-down block of apartments in the megacity of Lagos. Grandmommy is with Tola. But Moji and Dapo are locked down somewhere else in the city.

Lagos is one of the biggest cities on the African continent. Some people say more than twenty million people live in Lagos. Other people argue it is only fourteen million. Either way, Lagos is plenty bigger than London. And plenty bigger than New York. Lagos is a megacity!

But even a megacity cannot fight off the virus. Even a megacity has to go into lockdown. And millions of the people who live in Lagos have got to stay at home.

But Moji and Dapo are not at home anymore.

Tola wakes up on the morning after lockdown begins. She cannot hear engines revving, she cannot hear horns beeping, and she cannot hear the roar of the six lanes of traffic that usually pass by the apartments both day and night.

But through the open window Tola can hear the sound of a lot of people talking all at once.

Tola jumps out of bed and runs to the window. And there, on the rough ground outside the apartments, hawkers are setting up a market!

There are women selling tomatoes and onions. There are women selling bags of rice and bags of garri. There are women selling packets of bread and tins of sardines. There are women selling everything!

"Look, Grandmommy!" Tola points.

Grandmommy leans out of the window.

"Mama Taiwo!" she calls down. "What brings you here?"

A woman wearing a bright-red headscarf looks up.

"The police have chased us from our usual place," she calls back.

"Go home! Go home!" A voice suddenly erupts from another window.

It is Mama Business.

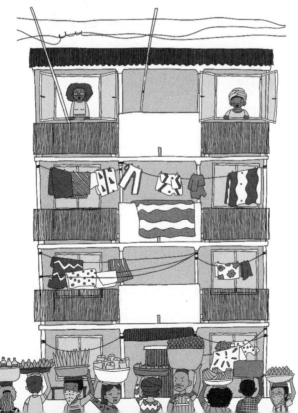

"It is lockdown!" she shouts. "Go home!"

"Lockdown is for people with money!" one of the hawkers shouts back.

"The police will chase you home!" Mama Business screeches. "De governor say LOCK DOWN!"

"Are you the governor?" Mama Taiwo demands with her hands on her hips.

Just then two police cars arrive. Police officers spill out, waving their batons. They order the hawkers to leave. And when the hawkers resist, the police chase them away.

"You see! I told you!" Mama Business shouts triumphantly.

But Grandmommy turns away from the window with a sad face. "How will they manage?" she mutters.

"Who?" asks Tola.

"Mama Taiwo and the others," she says. "They need a way to feed their children."

Grandmommy sits down with a sigh.

"Mama Business's family," she says, "send her money from abroad. So she can forget the problems of people who are not so lucky."

Tola knows that they are lucky too. Her father sends money from abroad to help them to pay the rent.

"We have plenty." Grandmommy nods.

She points. To a small sack of rice that is nearly full. To some stockfish. And to a few onions and tomatoes.

"Plenty to keep us going until Dapo sends money," Grandmommy says. "And I have the money for the rent safe and sound."

Tola looks at the tin where the money is kept. She rests her cheek on Grandmommy's arm.

The day passes slowly in their hot room. So does the next day, and the next day, and the next. Tola concentrates on her math. And when she is tired Grandmommy tells her stories about animals who can walk and talk. The tortoise stories are Tola's favorite. Tortoise is so clever he can even win a race against a rabbit.

The hawkers keep coming back. But the police keep coming back too. Tola is sad that the police do not care that the hawkers are hungry.

"Oh no!" Grandmommy explains. "It is not that they do not care. But the police are hungry too—so they have to do their job."

Tola thinks about this. It is another equation. But it must be possible to find a better one, one where nobody is hungry on either side.

Every day now, Tola's eyes rest on their food.

There is less and less each day. There is only rice left now.

Watching the sack of rice is like watching a number being subtracted again and again and again. This will lead to a zero in the end—or a negative number. Zero food will not fill her belly. And negative food will not either.

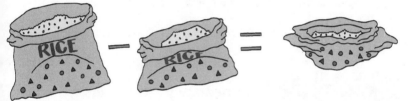

The day they finish the rice, Tola tries to concentrate on her math but she cannot. Why has Dapo not sent money?

"Do you think something has happened to Dapo?" Tola asks in a small voice.

Grandmommy shakes her head.

"Dapo is fine, I am sure," she says. "Maybe there are no cars for him to repair. Or maybe his boss says he must stay there for lockdown."

"Maybe he will not come until lockdown is finished?" Tola asks.

Her stomach growls. Grandmommy does not answer but she frowns. She gets out her phone. She hands it to Tola.

"Text your father," she says. "Tell him we need money."

Tola writes the text for Grandmommy because Grandmommy cannot read or write.

The answer comes immediately. Tola reads it aloud:

"I am sorry, Ma. Nobody is using my taxi because of lockdown. I have no money to send. I am praying that you and the children will be OK."

Tola stares at Grandmommy. What will they do now? She is too hungry to think properly.

Grandmommy and Tola sit without speaking.

Then they hear the hawkers come back to the rough ground.

"Take money from the tin," Grandmommy says. "Go and buy garri from the hawkers."

Tola gasps.

The tin is where the rent money is kept safely until the landlord comes to collect it. What will happen if he comes and there is no money there to pay?

"We will eat only once a day," Grandmommy says. "That way we will not spend too much. And we can replenish the tin when Dapo sends money."

So Tola creeps out of the apartments to buy a small bag of garri. Garri is like oats. Tola

and Grandmommy eat it cold mixed with water so they don't have to spend money on fuel for the stove ring.

Tola is still hungry. Her stomach still hurts. But she does not complain.

Now to pass the time Grandmommy tells Tola Bible stories. Tola likes the stories about Moses best. Tola has given up thinking about math. It is too hard to think when you are hungry.

Sometimes, when Tola smells the neighbors' food cooking, she creeps down the corridor just to smell it.

Mrs. Abdul's food always smells the best. Mr. Abdul goes out to work every day. Sometimes, the police see him and chase him back. And sometimes, they don't. But somehow, he earns enough to feed his family.

One day, Mrs. Abdul opens her door while Tola is leaning against it, breathing in the smell of savory beans. Tola falls into the room.

"Tola!" Mrs. Abdul cries.

Tola scrambles up.

"What is it?" Mrs. Abdul asks kindly. "Is something wrong?"

"No." Tola shakes her head. Then she blurts out, "Your food smells good."

Mrs. Abdul smiles.

"It is only beans," she says.

Tola's stomach growls. Mrs. Abdul looks at her with a small frown.

"Are you hungry?" she asks.

Tola shakes her head. Grandmommy always says never to beg from the neighbors. Quickly, she runs back to their room.

That evening, Mr. Abdul knocks on Tola and Grandmommy's door.

"Mr. Abdul!" Grandmommy exclaims.

"Come in! Come in! How are you and the family?"

"Thank you, Mama Mighty, thank you," Mr. Abdul says. "*Hamdulillah*, we are all well. And how are you?"

"You see us here," Grandmommy says— because that is as much as they have to be thankful for right now.

Mr. Abdul nods. His eyes glance toward the corner of the room where there is usually a sack of rice or a basket of yams. It is empty.

Then Grandmommy asks, "Did you manage to work today? The police did not chase you back?"

"Not today!" Mr. Abdul laughs. "*Hamdulillah!*"

"Your customers still want clothes?" Grandmommy asks.

"Of course!" Mr. Abdul says. "Some people are so rich they are spending lockdown sitting at home planning new outfits!"

Grandmommy and Tola shake their heads in wonder.

"I have these customers," Mr. Abdul
continues. "Very rich. Very, very rich. But they
still have their problems."

"What kind of problems?" Grandmommy
asks incredulously.

"Their house girl has gone back to her
village," Mr. Abdul says. "She thinks she will be
safe from the coronavirus there."

Grandmommy snorts.

"So now they have no one to clean their house and help their cook to chop the vegetables," Mr. Abdul says.

"What about the owner?" Grandmommy asks. "Can she not clean her own house and prepare her own food?"

Solemnly, Mr. Abdul shakes his head.

"Her nails are too long," he says. "They must be at least five inches. I am surprised she can even eat!"

Grandmommy laughs. And Tola giggles.

"So you see their problem," Mr. Abdul sighs. "They are good people. They feed the people who work for them well-well. They have enough food to feed one hundred house girls! Every time I go there, I smell fries and pizza or amala and ewedu—"

Tola's stomach growls so loudly it interrupts Mr. Abdul.

All of a sudden, Mr. Abdul looks at Tola.

"Maybe you want to
work there and eat their food?"

Tola shakes her head. But Mr. Abdul
reaches out and holds up Tola's arm.

"Too skinny," he says. "That food would
make you nice and fat! And you could send
home money for your grandmother too."

Tola looks at Grandmommy. Grandmommy
sucks her teeth.

"Who says I need money?" she asks. "Who
says we need food?"

"Oh well," Mr. Abdul says, standing up.
"I will tell Moses tomorrow that I did not find
a girl for him."

"Moses!" Tola exclaims.

"That is the name of the cook there," Mr. Abdul says. "He is a good man. And a good cook!"

"Moses is in the Bible!" Tola says.

Mr. Abdul smiles.

"He is in the Koran too," he says.

"And in the Torah," says Grandmommy.

"We have the same God." Mr. Abdul smiles.

"The same merciful God." Grandmommy nods.

"*Hamdulillah,*" Mr. Abdul says, and goes out.

Tola and Grandmommy look at each other. Then Tola looks at the tin. The money in there is less every day. And what will they do when it is all gone? What will they eat then? And what will happen when the landlord comes? He will chase them away. And where will they live when they have no money?

Tola bites her lip.

"We need money," she whispers.

"No!" Grandmommy frowns so hard her eyebrows cover her eyes. "How can I look after you if you are someplace else? How will I know if you are OK?"

Tola puts her hand on Grandmommy's arm. But Grandmommy does not look up.

Tola's stomach rumbles. Grandmommy raises her head then.

"You are hungry," she says.

Tola nods with tears in her eyes.

"If you go to work for that Moses, you will be able to eat plenty-plenty," Grandmommy says. "Mr. Abdul said so and he is a truthful man."

Tola's stomach growls again.

"You will grow fat and strong," Grandmommy whispers.

"And you will be able to pay the rent," Tola whispers too. "The landlord will not drive you from here."

Grandmommy puts her arms around Tola.

And Tola holds on to Grandmommy. She holds tight to Grandmommy all night. Far too tight to let go.

But in the morning, Tola is standing with Grandmommy outside Mr. Abdul's door. Tola is carrying a bag with her spare dress and her math notebook.

"They are good people," Mr. Abdul says, looking at Grandmommy. "You are doing the right thing."

Grandmommy says nothing.

Tola is holding tight to Grandmommy's hand. Far too tight to let go.

But she knows that if she does not let go there will only be more subtraction and no chance of addition or multiplication. And then, one day, there will be nothing left at all.

So very, very slowly Tola lets go of Grandmommy's hand.

And very, very quickly Mr. Abdul puts Tola on the back of his big black bicycle. And very, very quickly he rides away. That way Tola does not see Grandmommy cry.

Tola leans her head against Mr. Abdul's back. She cannot believe this is happening.

Mr. Abdul tells Tola the place she is going is a good place. He tells Tola that the people there are kind. He tells Tola that there will be plenty of food for her and plenty of money to send to Grandmommy.

Tola does not care. She just wants to be with Grandmommy. But she does not ask Mr. Abdul to stop pedaling. She does not tell him to turn back.

Mr. Abdul avoids the big roads where the police are stopping everybody.

Those roads used to be full of people shopping and jostling one another. Now people stare silently from their windows.

Mr. Abdul turns onto a bridge to the islands. The Carter Bridge. There are police blocking the way. Tola grips the bicycle tightly. The police have long guns in their arms.

Mr. Abdul stops the bicycle and holds up a piece of paper. A police officer comes to frown at it. He waves them through.

"One of my customers is a chief of police,"
Mr. Abdul says. "He has given me a pass. But
sometimes, the police cannot read it."

Tola says nothing. If that police officer had
not been able to read, then they would have
had to go home. And that would have been
wonderful . . . And bad.

Soon Mr. Abdul is pedaling along wide streets with high white walls and tall trees peeping over those walls. Tola can hear the roar of generators coming from every compound, making light for people rich enough to make their own electricity.

Mr. Abdul stops outside some metal gates. Through the gates Tola can see a house made of glass. And she recognizes it!

This is where Tola and Dapo came when Mr. Abdul broke his leg and they were delivering things to his customers.

"The Diamonds!" Tola exclaims.

This is the home of the famous Diamond couple whose Afrobeat music makes the whole country dance!

"You will be a celebrity when you come home!" Mr. Abdul smiles.

Soon a short man in a white uniform and a tall hat is hurrying from the glass house toward them.

Mr. Abdul lifts Tola off the bicycle.

"Alhaji!" the man calls to Mr. Abdul.

"Moses, how are you?" Mr. Abdul replies.

"I cannot complain," the man says. "And your family, nko?"

"*Hamdulillah*, they are well." Mr. Abdul nods his thanks.

"Is this the girl?" Moses peers at Tola. "She looks too small."

Tola stares at Moses. He might be in the Bible and the Koran and the Torah, but that did not mean that he was allowed to be rude!

"I am small but I am strong," Tola says crossly. "In fact, I am mighty."

Moses's eyebrows shoot up. Mr. Abdul laughs.

"She can clean the kitchen, floor, toilet—everything," he says. "And her eko is better than my wife's own."

"Is that so?" Moses asks.

He stares down at Tola for a while. Then he takes out an envelope full of money and gives it to Mr. Abdul. Mr. Abdul counts it carefully.

"I will give it to your grandmother," he says to Tola.

Tola nods. Once Mr. Abdul trusted her to collect money for him. Now she trusts Mr. Abdul to take her money safely to Grandmommy. And she knows Grandmommy trusts him too.

Then Moses says, "O-ya, Small-and-Mighty, follow me!"

He turns back toward the house.

Tola grips Mr. Abdul's robe.

"Go with Moses," Mr. Abdul says softly.

But Tola cannot let go.

Mr. Abdul has to loosen her hand. She lets him. And she lets him push her forward gently.

"Go on," he says. "I will come and see you soon."

Very, very quickly Mr. Abdul pedals away. That way, Tola does not see the tears in his eyes.

So Tola runs after Moses. There is a big, hard lump in her throat. And she cannot swallow it.

She follows Moses down a path past the glass house to a small, plain, ugly concrete building at the back of the compound.

"You must stay here," Moses says. "Until we know you do not have the virus."

Moses opens a door into the ugly building.

Inside is a tiny, clean room with a mat rolled in a corner. Hanging on the wall are two small dresses that look stiff and smart like Moses's uniform.

"This is your room," he says.

"What is this?" an old woman's voice asks crossly.

Tola turns around.

Coming out from another door in the building is a skinny old woman with strong arms.

"The new house girl," Moses answers. "Small-and-Mighty."

The old woman sucks her teeth.

"We will see about that!" she says.

Moses chuckles and walks away.

The old woman turns her back and starts to fill huge tubs with water from the tap.

All of a sudden Tola feels totally alone.

Grandmommy is far away. Moji is far away. Dapo is far away.

Suddenly, Tola's legs are so weak she almost falls down. She goes into her room and closes the door. Then she cries and cries and cries.

When she stops crying, there is silence.

The only thing she can hear is water splashing. It sounds like someone is washing clothes.

Slowly Tola gets up and opens her door a crack. The old woman is washing a mountain of clothes in the big plastic tubs. It looks like hard work.

Tola watches for a while.

Then she asks in a small voice, "Can I help you, Ma?"

"This work is too heavy for someone so small!" the old woman grunts.

She is struggling to wring out a heavy sheet.

Tola goes to squat on the other side of the big tub. She takes the other end of the heavy sheet and twists with all her might.

The old woman looks surprised. And pleased.

In the evening, Moses comes back carrying big bowls of eba and stockfish stew. He stops and stares.

Tola is elbow-deep in the tubs—washing and rinsing and washing and rinsing the wet, heavy clothes.

And the old woman is resting on a stool talking nonstop about her fourteen children who are all good-for-nothing.

Tola looks up and sees Moses staring. The old woman looks up too.

"Why so surprised?" she cackles. "You told me yourself she was mighty!"

Moses laughs.

"O-ya, Small-but-Mighty, come and eat," he says.

Tola jumps up. She misses Grandmommy so much that her heart is sore and swollen—like her eyes after all that crying.

But tonight she will eat plenty-plenty and Grandmommy will eat plenty too!

Tola Gets Tough

Once upon a time, Tola lived in a run-down block of apartments with her clever sister, her busy brother, and her kind and grumpy grandmother.

Now Tola sleeps alone in a room made of concrete and works in a house made of glass. She works with Moses and an old woman called Mama Useless.

Every day Tola wakes when the roosters begin to crow. The sky is still dark. How do the roosters know the sun is on the way? Tola wonders.

She washes at the outside tap, hurries into her uniform, and runs up to the glass house. It is as big as a palace! Each time Tola enters, she looks around in awe!

Marble floors spread in every direction. Bronze masks stare down from every wall. Wooden friezes of the oba kings divide every room. It is like the Lagos museum where Tola went once with Moji.

But this is a house, not a museum. And keeping a house as big as a palace clean is hard work! Scrubbing the floors makes Tola's back ache, reaching up to dust

the masks and friezes makes her arms tired, washing so many sinks and toilets and bathrooms makes her hands sting.

And when Moses gives her piles of food, she eats and eats and eats. Fried plantain and chicken and crayfish moi-moi!

"I hope you clean as well as you eat," Moses grumbles.

But he does not find any dirt on the floors or dust on the statues or stains in the bathrooms.

"Your grandmother trained you well," he admits. "You know how to clean!"

But cleaning is not all that Tola knows.

The stool where Tola sits to eat in the kitchen is next to a pile of papers. The papers list all the deliveries made to the house. All the food delivered to the kitchen, all the diesel delivered for the generator, all the chemicals delivered for the swimming pool, all the plants delivered for the garden. Next to each item on the list is its price and at the bottom of the list is the total cost.

While Tola is sitting in the kitchen, she likes to total the numbers on the lists in her head—and then check the figure at the bottom of each page to see if she got it right.

"Those are Oga's important papers!" Moses warns her. "Don't let him catch you touching them!"

Luckily, the first time Mr. Diamond comes into the kitchen, Tola is not holding the papers. Still she jumps!

Mr. Diamond is wearing a white tracksuit without a single stain and a heavy gold chain that shines like the sun. But the look on his face is the look of an angry thunder god as he picks up the papers. His eyes flash like he could set them ablaze with lightning!

"Did all of this get delivered?" he asks angrily.

"Yes, sa." Moses nods.

"Why does this house cost me so much?" Mr. Diamond roars as he marches out of the kitchen.

Moses and Tola look at each other.

"It is expensive to be rich." Moses shrugs.

And Tola giggles.

Later, when she is cleaning upstairs, she overhears Mr. and Mrs. Diamond arguing. They are shouting so loud Tola can hear every word.

"Children need their mother!" Mrs.
Diamond screams.

"I am giving them every—
opportunity—in—life!" Mr.
Diamond roars back. "Is that not
good enough for you?"

"No!" Mrs. Diamond
screams. "Not when
they need their mother."

Doors slam. Tola
jumps. The rest of the
day the house is in silence.
No words and no music. Just
lonely crying from inside the
bedroom of Mrs. Diamond.

"Where are the children?" Tola asks
Mama Useless later.

"What children?" The old woman frowns.

"Oga and Madam's children," Tola says.
"I never see them."

"Why would you see them?" Mama Useless sucks her teeth. "They are in London."

Tola's eyebrows raise high on her head.

"Alone?" she asks. "So far?"

"In boarding school," Mama Useless says.

That night, when Tola is crying for Grandmommy, she remembers the lonely crying of Mrs. Diamond. She is missing people too!

Having money does not mean having no problems at all, Tola realizes. Being rich does not solve all the equations.

Just then—in the shed right next to Tola's room—the generator comes on with a roar. It comes on every time the electricity goes out.

In Nigeria, electricity is not on all the time. Sometimes it cuts out for a few minutes, or a few hours, or a few days.

If you are poor, there is nothing you can do to charge your phone or keep your food fresh.

But rich people have generators to make electricity for them when the main supply goes off.

Diesel for the generator is the Diamonds' top household expense. When Tola first read the diesel figures, she choked. Mr. Diamond spends more money on diesel in a month than Grandmommy spends on rent in a year!

And that is an equation that seems unfair, Tola thinks as she goes to sleep.

The next morning, as Tola is washing at the tap, she notices a small bush growing outside the generator shed. She had not noticed it before because it had no flowers. But now it does! And its flowers are just opening. Tola goes to look. The flowers smell so good they make Tola smile!

Tola notices then, too, that the generator shed door is open. Inside is the generator with numbers written on its side. Tola cannot resist numbers! She creeps in to read them.

They tell her how much power the generator can make and how much diesel it can guzzle in one hour. Numbers can explain the whole world.

Later, when Tola is cleaning upstairs in the big glass house, she hears the lonely crying again. It makes her heart hurt. She wishes she could make Mrs. Diamond smile.

Suddenly, Tola puts down her scrubbing brush and slips out of the house.

Late in the afternoon, when Mrs. Diamond comes out of her room, she finds a branch of sweet-smelling flowers lying on the floor outside her door.

Mrs. Diamond is still smiling when she comes downstairs. She goes straight to her husband and puts her arms around him.

Mr. Diamond is so surprised he jumps.

"I know you want to do what's best for the children," she says.

Mr. Diamond says nothing, then he puts his arms around Mrs. Diamond too.

"I know you miss the children," he says.

And then they both smile! Peeping around the kitchen door, Tola grins.

"Come and eat!" Moses growls. "And mind your own business."

So Tola does. She sits on her stool and thinks about the flowers growing outside the generator shed that made Mrs. Diamond smile. She thinks about the numbers on the generator inside and about the numbers on the papers she had added up.

Suddenly, Tola sits up straight.

"Moses!" Tola cries. "The numbers!"

"Don't bother me now," Moses says with his back to her. "I am cooking."

But Tola is standing up now. Her brain is whirring. And it will not stop.

"They are cheating him!" she cries. "They are cheating Mr. Diamond!"

"Who is cheating me?" roars a voice.

Moses and Tola whirl around. And there is Mr. Diamond standing in the doorway with his thunder-god face. Mrs. Diamond is behind him.

Tola's eyes open wide with fright. She looks at Moses but he only frowns.

"Answer the oga!" Moses points his spoon at Tola.

Tola opens her mouth. But nothing comes out. The roaring has scared off all her words too!

"Speak!" Mr. Diamond bellows.

But all the figures in Tola's head have whirred away in fright.

"How can the child speak when you are shouting like that?"

Mrs. Diamond pushes past her husband and bends toward Tola.

"It is OK," she says. "You can tell me."

70

And Mrs. Diamond speaks so kindly that eventually Tola's voice comes out from where it was hiding.

"The numbers for the diesel," she whispers. "They are wrong."

Mr. Diamond frowns.

"How so?" he growls.

"Shhh!" Mrs. Diamond flaps her hand at him.

"On the papers," Tola whispers.

"You let her touch my receipts?" Mr. Diamond growls at Moses.

"Shhh!" Mrs. Diamond looks at her husband crossly.

"It is OK," she says again to Tola. "You are not in trouble."

Mr. Diamond snorts.

Mrs. Diamond turns around and raises her eyebrows until Mr. Diamond steps back and is quiet.

"Go on, Tola," says Mrs. Diamond. "You can explain."

So Tola whispers the amount of diesel that is delivered to the house every month. Then she whispers the numbers on the generator that say how much diesel it uses every hour. Then Tola explains that even if the generator was running for twenty-four hours every single day of the month, it could not use even half of the diesel that the papers say is delivered every month.

Mr. Diamond leaps in the air as if a snake has bitten him on the bottom. He snatches up the papers and examines them himself.

"Thieves!" he shouts. "Robbers! Liars!"

And this time Mrs. Diamond does not shush him.

"I knew that they were cheating me!" he yells. "I knew it."

Mr. Diamond gets out his phone but Moses interrupts him.

"Sa! Sa!" he says. "They are coming now-now!"

"What?" Mr. Diamond frowns at him.

"The tanker is coming today!" Moses says. "Always first Tuesday they come!"

"I will arrest the driver!" Mr. Diamond threatens.

Mrs. Diamond shakes her head.

"How can you arrest him?" She smiles. "Are you a police officer?"

"No," says Mr. Diamond. "But I know someone who is!"

He speed dials a number on his phone.

"Kunle! Kunle!" he shouts. "There are some big thieves coming to my place. Big-big thieves. You better get here double quick."

Mrs. Diamond takes out her own phone.

"Maybe we can sort this out with the diesel company," she says.

Mrs. Diamond speaks to whoever answers the phone. She explains the whole problem.

Whoever she is speaking to argues back.

Mr. Diamond snatches the phone.

"I will arrest your driver!" he yells into the phone. "I will take your whole tanker!"

Then he cuts off the call.

And just at that moment, a loud horn blows at the gates of the glass house. It is the diesel tanker!

Mr. Diamond runs out of the kitchen. Moses races after him, waving his wooden spoon. Mrs. Diamond grabs Tola's hand and runs up the path. When Mama Useless sees them pass, she too follows.

The tanker driver is opening the gates when Mr. Diamond gets there. He jumps up into the open cab and snatches the keys.

"WHAT IS THIS?" the driver cries. "Give me my keys!"

"LIAR! THIEF! THIEF!" Mr. Diamond screeches.

"Who are you calling a thief?" the driver yells. "I will fight you now-now!"

Mr. Diamond looks like he is going to punch the driver. But just then, a police car speeds up to the gates. Police officers with masks on leap out.

Tola is surprised to see the masks. She has been stuck

inside for so long she has forgotten all about masks.

"What is happening here?" one of the police officers asks.

The driver starts telling them how Mr. Diamond has stolen his keys.

But Mr. Diamond gives the police officer the keys to the tanker.

"Kunle, they have overcharged me billions for my diesel," he explains.

"I just deliver the diesel. And hand over the receipt." The driver holds up his hands. "I am not a thief!"

Suddenly, Tola sees Mr. Abdul riding down the street on his bike. He is coming to see her! But at the sight of the police cars and the tanker, Mr. Abdul stops with his mouth open.

It opens even wider when a big golden BMW screeches past him. A man jumps out wearing an agbada embroidered with gold.

"Take your hands off my man!" he snaps at the police officers.

"You!" Mr. Diamond jabs his finger six feet from the man's chest. "You have been stealing from me!"

"Nonsense!" The embroidered man flicks his hand as if he is brushing Mr. Diamond's finger away. "You have no proof of anything!"

Mrs. Diamond steps forward.

"Our girl," she says, "can prove everything!"

Tola tries to hide behind Mama Useless. But the old woman pushes Tola forward.

Everybody stares at Tola. The embroidered man laughs.

"A house girl?" he snorts. "What does she know?"

Tola looks down at the ground. It is true. She is only a house girl.

"She is a good girl," Moses says loudly.

"A clever girl," the old woman says.

"The best girl," adds Mr. Abdul.

"And our girl," growls Mr. Diamond.

"We have complete faith in her," says Mrs. Diamond firmly.

She holds out the receipts to Tola.

"Prove it, Tola," she says.

Tola is so surprised she takes the papers.

"Here is the one . . ." she whispers.

"Speak up!" says the chief police officer.

"Here is the one . . ." Tola tries again.

"The receipt," says Mrs. Diamond.

"The receipt," Tola says, "from January for diesel. Here is the one from February and the one from March. Each one is for the same amount of diesel."

"So?" the embroidered man asks rudely.

Tola's hands are shaking. But she continues to speak.

"The generator here uses one gallon of diesel per hour," she says.

The embroidered man starts to fidget. "Why are we listening to a small girl?" he complains.

"Quiet!" snaps the chief police officer.

Tola swallows.

"Continue," the police officer says to Tola.

"Go on!" Mrs. Diamond smiles.

So Tola goes on.

"The generator uses one gallon of diesel per hour at full capacity. So if it was on twenty-four hours a day, then it would use twenty-four gallons a day. If it was on all day every day for a month, it would use 744 gallons maximum. But the receipt is for fifteen hundred gallons delivered each month. That is more than twice what the generator could use."

"NONSENSE!" the embroidered man screams. "How can anyone prove what a generator uses?"

"It says on the machine," says Tola.

The embroidered man suddenly runs toward his car.

"Stop him!" barks the chief police officer.

Mr. Abdul sticks out his foot. The embroidered man trips over it and falls—*bam!*— on the ground!

The police officers pull him up and handcuff him.

"Quick work," they say to Mr. Abdul.

"Now show me the generator," the chief police officer says.

So Tola leads everybody to the generator shed. She shows them the numbers on the generator and the numbers on the papers. The chief police officer studies them and nods.

"She is correct!" he says.

And Mr. Abdul, Mama Useless, and Moses all cheer.

Then the embroidered man is bundled into the police car. "Thank you, Kunle! Thank you!" Mr. Diamond says to the chief police officer.

The chief police officer laughs.

"It is not me you should thank!" he says. "It is this young lady."

When Tola realizes that the chief police officer is talking about her, she hides behind Mr. Abdul.

"She should have a reward!" Mrs. Diamond says.

"She deserves one." The police officer nods.

"A reward is ten percent," says Mama Useless.

Mr. Diamond splutters.

But he pulls out his wallet and counts out some notes.

He holds them out to Tola. Her eyes are wide. Her heart is pounding. There are enough notes there for Grandmommy to pay the rent for three whole years!

"Take them," Mrs. Diamond laughs.

Mr. Abdul plucks Tola from behind him and pushes her forward.

Tola curtsies to Mr. Diamond.

"Thank you, sa," she says. "Thank you, thank you, thank you, thank you."

Tola knows how happy Grandmommy will be. All her worries will be over!

Tola gives the money to Mr. Abdul. He is her old, old friend.

"Give this to Grandmommy," she says. "For the rent."

Slowly, Mr. Abdul takes the money.

"Your grandmother will be so proud of you," he says.

Suddenly, the pain of missing Grandmommy is so strong that Tola cries out.

"Tola, what is wrong?" Mrs. Diamond asks. "What is paining you?"

"I want to go home," Tola cries.

Mr. and Mrs. Diamond look surprised.

"Why?" Mr. Diamond cries. "Did I not just give you money?"

"Children need more than money!" Mama Useless glares at Mr. Diamond. "They need to live with people—the people who love them most."

The chief police officer nods. "That is the best way for children to grow strong," he says.

Mr. and Mrs. Diamond look at each other. Then Mrs. Diamond looks at Tola.

"You can go home, Tola," she says, smiling sadly.

Tola looks at her with wide eyes. She claps her hands together.

But Mr. Diamond says, "This is ridiculous.

She cannot go! She is our house girl."

"We will find another one," Mrs. Diamond says.

"I need this one," says Mr. Diamond. "I need her to check the receipts every week!"

Mr. Abdul takes Tola's hand.

"I will bring her back once a week to do your papers, sa," he says.

"Abi?" Mr. Abdul looks down at Tola.

"Yes, sa." Tola nods so hard her neck hurts. "I will come back to do the numbers."

"Of course we will pay her." Mrs. Diamond smiles.

"One day," the chief police officer says to Tola, "you might become an accountant."

Mama Useless snorts. "This child is so mighty she will figure out the numbers so we can fly to Mars and back in the blink of any eye," she says.

Tola has never thought of numbers so big.

Her eyes grow so wide that everyone laughs.

"Go and collect your things," says Mr. Abdul, patting her shoulder.

Tola runs to collect her things from her room, then rushes back to say goodbye.

She throws her arms around the old woman.

"Thank you," she says. "I hope your children come to look after you."

Then Tola turns to Moses. "Thank you," she says. "I hope the next girl is good."

Tola curtsies to Mr. and Mrs. Diamond. "I hope you get your own children back," she says.

Tears spring into Mrs. Diamond's eyes. Mr. Diamond looks thoughtful.

Then Mr. Abdul puts Tola on the back of the big black bicycle once again. And he pedals off.

"Let's go home!" he says.

"Home!" Tola echoes.

"Moji and Dapo are not back yet," Mr. Abdul warns. "They have to wait for lockdown to be finished."

Tola nods sadly.

"But Grandmommy is there," Mr. Abdul says.

Tola's heart makes a happy jump.

Coronavirus ko, coronavirus ni, Tola cannot help smiling.

She is heading toward home. Toward the person who loves her best in all the world. And the person she loves best too.